MATT AND

YUCK

YUCK'S SLIME MONSTER
AND
YUCK'S GROSS PARTY

Illustrated by Nigel Baines

A Paula Wiseman Book

Simon & Schuster Books for Young Readers

New York   London   Toronto   Sydney   New Delhi

**FOR
SLIME MONSTERS:**

Venetia You Ingrid
Geoff Kate
Kat Jo Elisa
Margaret Heather

SIMON & SCHUSTER BOOKS FOR YOUNG READERS
An imprint of Simon & Schuster Children's Publishing Division
1230 Avenue of the Americas, New York, New York 10020
This book is a work of fiction. Any references to historical events,
real people, or real locales are used fictitiously. Other names, characters,
places, and incidents are products of the author's imagination, and
any resemblance to actual events or locales or persons,
living or dead, is entirely coincidental.
Text copyright © 2007 by Matthew Morgan and David Sinden
Illustrations copyright © 2007 by Nigel Baines
Originally published in Great Britain in 2007 by Simon & Schuster UK, Ltd.
First US edition May 2012
SIMON & SCHUSTER BOOKS FOR YOUNG READERS
is a trademark of Simon & Schuster, Inc.
For information about special discounts for bulk purchases, please contact
Simon & Schuster Special Sales at 1-866-506-1949 or
business@simonandschuster.com.
The Simon & Schuster Speakers Bureau can bring authors to your
live event. For more information or to book an event, contact the
Simon & Schuster Speakers Bureau at 1-866-248-3049 or
visit our website at www.simonspeakers.com.
Also available in a Simon & Schuster Books for Young Readers
hardcover edition
The text for this book is set in Bembo.
The illustrations for this book are rendered in pencil and ink.
Manufactured in the United States of America
0312 OFF
2 4 6 8 10 9 7 5 3 1
Cataloging-in-Publication data for this book is available from the Library
of Congress.
ISBN 978-1-4424-5124-7 (hc)
ISBN 978-1-4424-5126-1 (pbk)
ISBN 978-1-4424-5173-5 (eBook)
yuckweb.com

CAUTION:
YUCKY FUN INSIDE!

YUCK'S SLIME MONSTER

"Yuck, look what you've done!"

Polly Princess stood in Yuck's bedroom doorway clutching her *Glitter Girl* magazine. The pages were sticky and sloppy and covered in slime.

"It wasn't me," Yuck said. "I didn't touch your silly magazine." He was lying on his bed reading *Oink*. He turned the page. . . .

2

Polly whacked Yuck with her slimy copy of *Glitter Girl*. "Don't you dare touch my magazine again!"

"But it wasn't me."

"Then who was it?"

Yuck got out of bed and put *Oink* in his school bag.

"It must have been the Slime Monster," he said. Yuck held his arms out in front of him like a Slime Monster and stomped in a circle.

"There's no such thing as a Slime Monster," Polly said. "It was you and your slugs."

She opened the lid of Yuck's desk and peered inside. It was full of slugs.

"Hey, get your nose out of Slime City!"

Polly picked out a slug, threw it on the floor, and . . .

"Stop! Don't!" Yuck yelled.

Polly stepped on the slug.

SQUIDGE!

Polly raced out of the room.

Yuck looked at the squashed slug on his carpet. He scooped it up. Slime was leaking from the slug's body.

"Are you alive?" he said, stroking it.

The slug's antennae twitched feebly.

"You'll be okay. I'll fix you," Yuck said. "And then we'll fix Polly for what she did!"

Yuck raced downstairs with the slug in his hand.

Polly was waiting at the front door. "Hurry up, Yuck! I don't want to be late for school."

Yuck dashed past her and into the kitchen. He grabbed the first aid box from the shelf in the corner, took out a bandage, and wrapped it around the slug.

Mom was putting the breakfast things away. "What have you got there, Yuck?" she asked.

"My slug," Yuck told her. "His name's Hero. I'm making him better."

Yuck slipped the bandaged slug into his bag and left for school with Polly.

He arrived ten minutes late. Mrs. Wagon the Dragon was already pacing up and down at the front of the classroom.

Yuck opened the door quietly.

"Who's going to be in charge of Cuddly Corner this week?" the Dragon asked, pointing her umbrella.

Schoolie Julie put her hand up. "Me, Mrs. Wagon, please!"

Ben Bongo put his hand up. "Me, Mrs. Wagon!"

Yuck crept along the floor on all fours, past the line of desks.

"Late AGAIN, Yuck!" the Dragon said.

"Sorry, Mrs. Wagon," Yuck said, "there was an emergency."

The Dragon shot Yuck "the look." The sight of her glare sent Yuck sprawling back into his seat next to Little Eric.

Yuck sneaked the slug from his bag, unraveled its bandage, and showed it to Little Eric.

"What happened?" Little Eric whispered.

"Polly squashed him. But he's going to be okay," Yuck said. "His name's Hero."

"What's THAT you've got?" the Dragon boomed.

Yuck looked up. The Dragon was pointing her umbrella toward him.

"My slug, Mrs. Wagon," he said.

"Get it out of here at once! You're not to bring animals to class!"

"But Mrs.—"

The Dragon pointed at Yuck with her umbrella.

"If you want to play with animals, then you can look after Cuddly Corner!"

"But, Miss," Yuck said. "Cuddly Corner isn't any fun. There's only a hamster, and all it does is go round and round in its wheel. I like slugs and snails and worms and snakes."

The Dragon whacked Yuck's desk with her

umbrella. "Every day this week, before and after school, you're to clean the hamster's cage, give it some food, and change its water!"

"But, Mrs. Wagon, I—"

"No buts! All week you're to get to school early and leave last."

Yuck groaned.

"Now, face the front, everyone. It's time for your math test!"

Yuck straightened Hero out, bandaged him up, and slipped him back into his bag.

He pulled out his copy of *Oink* and opened it inside his math book, to read more about the Slime Monster.

Yuck decided that when he was EMPEROR OF EVERYTHING he would rename Cuddly Corner SLIME ZONE. Inside, the walls would be green and slimy. A Slime Monster would live there. And every lunchtime, Yuck would let it out to slime the school. . . .

At the end of the day he took the key

from the hook marked Cuddly Corner and walked to a hut at the edge of the playground. He undid the padlock on the door and went inside.

The hut smelled of hamster. A whirring sound was coming from a cage on a table in the corner. The hamster was running in its wheel.

Yuck peered through the bars of the cage and the hamster hopped down to see him.

"Haven't you got anyone to play with, Hammie?" Yuck asked.

The hamster twitched its whiskers.

"Do you want to have some fun?"

Hammie's whiskers twitched again.

"Then let's build a SLIME MACHINE!" Yuck said.

Hammie squeaked happily.

Yuck had never built a slime machine before, but he'd seen the one in *Oink*.

He opened the cage and took Hammie out, then fetched Hero from his bag. Yuck unwrapped the soggy bandage, and his slug started sliming across the table.

The hamster gave the slug a sniff.

"Hammie, this is Hero. Hero, this is Hammie," Yuck said.

Yuck placed Hammie's wheel on the table and wrapped one end of the soggy bandage around it. Then, from the corner of the hut, he fetched a bucket and threaded the other end of the bandage through its handle.

He tied both ends of the bandage together to make a loop.

"THIS is our slime machine!" he said.

Hammie hopped into the wheel.

"That's it, Hammie, you're going to be the engine. The bandage will be the conveyor belt that carries the slime."

Yuck placed Hero on the conveyor belt.

"Hero, you're going to be the slime-maker."

He dipped his finger into the bucket. The slime was cold and slippery.

PLOP! PLOP! PLOP!

With Hammie running happily in the wheel, and Hero sliming happily on the conveyor belt, Yuck crept out.

"Good night, Hammie. Good night, Hero," he said.

He locked the door and went home.

When he arrived, Polly was in the living room watching *Sparkle*.

"Can we watch *Grossout*?" Yuck asked.

"I was here first," Polly said.

"But I had to look after Cuddly Corner."

"Cuddly Corner? Why are you looking after Cuddly Corner—or did you run out of slugs to play with?"

Polly picked a crusty glob of Hero's slime from her shoe and flicked it at Yuck.

He caught the slime and wiped it on her hair, then ran to his room to read *Oink*.

20

The next morning, Yuck was the first to arrive at school.

"Rockits!" he said, opening the door to Cuddly Corner. The bucket was FULL of slime. All night Hammie had been turning the wheel, and all night Hero had been sliming on the conveyor belt.

The slime machine had worked!

"Well done, Hammie! Well done, Hero!"

He placed Hero on the table beside the cage, took Hammie out of the wheel, and gave them both some lettuce and fresh water. Then he untied the bandage, rolled it up, and hid it in the corner.

"I'll see you later. Have fun," he said.

Yuck headed outside carrying the bucket full of slime.

At lunch he slipped a handful of slime down Little Eric's shirt.

Little Eric felt something gooey running down his back.

"Urrgghh!" he said. "What's that?"

"Slime!" Yuck told him. He showed Little Eric the bucket.

"Let me have a try," Little Eric said. He took a big scoop of slime and flicked it at Yuck.

Yuck flicked a handful of slime back at Little Eric.

Then they both took another scoop and catapulted slime into the air.

"It's raining slime!" Yuck said.

At that moment, Polly Princess and Juicy Lucy skipped out of the cafeteria into the playground.

"URRGGHH!" Polly shrieked as slime rained down on her hair.

Lucy looked up, and slime dropped into her mouth. "AARRGGHH!" she screamed.

Yuck and Little Eric were giggling.

But just then, the Dragon marched over. "What's going on here?" she boomed, seeing Polly and Lucy covered in slime.

"It was Yuck!" Polly said.

Little Eric stood in front of the bucket to hide it.

"It wasn't us, Mrs. Wagon," Yuck said.

"Then who was it?" the Dragon asked.

"It was the Slime Monster, Mrs. Wagon," Yuck said. "It was horrible, like a human being, but slimier and scarier. And it walked funny, Mrs. Wagon—like this . . ."

Yuck held his arms out in front of him like a Slime Monster and stomped in a circle.

"What nonsense," the Dragon said.

"There's no such thing as a Slime Monster, Mrs. Wagon," Polly told her.

"I want everyone to get cleaned up immediately," the Dragon said. "When I find out who did this they'll be in BIG TROUBLE."

But for the rest of lunchtime, Yuck and

Little Eric went hunting for more slugs.

After school they took them all to Cuddly Corner.

Yuck fetched the bandage from the corner of the hut and looped one end of it around Hammie's wheel. This time he placed TWO buckets on the floor, and threaded the other end of the bandage through both their handles.

He tied the ends together, and the conveyor belt was ready.

"Wow!" Little Eric said. "A slime machine!"

Yuck placed Hero on the conveyor belt, then added the extra slugs behind him in a line.

"More slugs means more slime!" Yuck said.

Hammie hopped into the wheel and started running. The wheel turned, the conveyor belt moved, and the slime machine began sliming.

Plop! Plop!
Plop! Splat!

Hammie was running at full speed.

"That's it," Yuck said. "Keep it up."

He made sure all the slugs were in a neat line and copying Hero at the front.

"The slime will be ready in the morning," Yuck said to Little Eric. "Get here early."

They left and locked the door.

The next morning, Yuck and Little Eric rushed to school. They opened the door of Cuddly Corner and saw the TWO buckets full of slime.

The machine had been sliming all night.

"Well done, Hammie," Yuck said. "Well done, Hero. Well done, everyone!"

He took Hammie out of the wheel and placed Hero and the other slugs beside the cage, giving them lettuce and fresh water.

"We'll see you later. Have fun."

Yuck left carrying one bucket full of slime. Little Eric carried the other.

That lunchtime, Yuck and Little Eric poured the slime along the school corridor. They skidded up and down.

"Rockits!" Yuck said. "Slimeboarding!"

Fartin' Martin and Tom Butts ran over.

"Slime!" Tom Butts said. "Brilliant!"

"Let's have a turn!" Fartin' Martin said.

But at that moment, Polly and Lucy came out of Miss Fortune's classroom, each carrying a stack of books. Clip-Clop Chloe, Megan the Mouth, and Madison Snake came after them.

"Watch out!" Fartin' Martin called.

"Arrgghh!" Polly screamed.

"Help!" Lucy screamed.

Fartin' Martin and Tom Butts skidded toward them.

WHOOSH!

The books tumbled as everyone slid down the corridor and landed with a . . .

SPLAT!

Just as they struggled to their feet, Frank the Tank came running out of the bathroom. He slipped on the slime and slid down the corridor like a bowling ball.

CRASH!

He knocked everyone down like bowling pins.

The Dragon heard the noise and dashed out of her classroom.

"What's going on here?" she boomed. She slipped and landed on her bottom. "Where IS all this slime coming from?"

"It's the Slime Monster, Mrs. Wagon," Yuck said.

"Slime Monster!" everyone shrieked.

"W-w-what's a Slime Monster?" Frank the Tank asked.

"It's like a human being, but slimier and scarier," Yuck said. "And it walks funny— like this . . ."

Yuck held his arms out in front of him like a Slime Monster and stomped in a circle.

"He's lying. There's no such thing as a Slime Monster," Polly said.

The Dragon clambered to her feet. She scowled at Yuck. "If I find out this has anything to do with you, you'll be in BIG TROUBLE. Go and get a mop from Mr. Sweep and clean this up. You too, Eric."

"But it wasn't us, Mrs. Wagon," Little Eric said. "It was—"

"I'll hear no more nonsense about Slime Monsters!" the Dragon said.

Yuck and Little Eric giggled as the Dragon squelched back into her classroom.

"Is there really a Slime Monster sliming the school?" Frank the Tank asked.

"Yes," Yuck said. "If you TOUCH the Slime Monster, your skin melts."

"If you HEAR the Slime Monster, your earwax melts," Little Eric said.

"And if you SEE the Slime Monster, you have to . . . RUN FOR YOUR LIFE!"

Yuck and Little Eric laughed all the way to Mr. Sweep's closet. There, beside the mop, they found more buckets.

After school, Yuck, Fartin' Martin, Tom Butts, and Little Eric went hunting for slugs again, filling their pockets before heading to Cuddly Corner.

Yuck fetched the bandage, and this time threaded the conveyor belt through TEN buckets.

"Cool! A slime machine!" Tom Butts said.

"Awesome!" Fartin' Martin said.

Yuck placed Hero at the front of the conveyor belt. Everyone took the slugs from their pockets and lined them up behind him. Hammie hopped into the wheel.

"Run, Hammie, run!"

The machine began sliming.

PLoP! PLoP! PLoP! PLoP! SPLAT! PLoP! PLoP! Gurgle! SPLAT! PLoP!

"We'll collect the slime in the morning!" Yuck said.

The next morning, Yuck, Fartin' Martin, Tom Butts, and Little Eric arrived at school early. They ran to Cuddly Corner.

Inside were TEN buckets FULL of slime!

"Well done, Hammie," Yuck said. "Well done, Hero. Well done, everyone!"

He placed Hammie and the slugs in a huddle and gave them lettuce and fresh water. Then he took the bandage off the machine and hid it.

Yuck, Fartin' Martin, Tom Butts, and Little Eric picked up the buckets full of slime and set to work.

"Let's let the Slime Monster loose," Yuck said.

At lunchtime they slimed the classrooms. They slimed windows and whiteboards, door handles and desks, books and bags.

When the Dragon sat on her chair, it squelched. She opened her umbrella as slime dripped from the ceiling.

They slimed the toilet seats and sinks.

They slimed the pizzas and puddings in the cafeteria.

"There's a Slime Monster on the loose!" Ben Bongo cried, about to eat a spoonful of slime.

Everyone ran out to the playground.

But the playground was slimy too!

Megan the Mouth slipped off the jungle gym and Spoiled Jessica *whooshed* down the slide.

Mr. Reaper, the principal, was on playground patrol.

"Where IS all this slime coming from?" he asked.

"It's the Slime Monster," everyone said. "The Slime Monster's come to get us!"

"There's no such thing as a Slime Monster!" Polly cried. She was sitting up in a tree with Lucy, trying to escape from the slime.

Meanwhile, Yuck, Fartin' Martin, Tom Butts, and Little Eric were collecting more slugs.

"Let's use snails, too," Yuck said, filling his bag. "We're going to make the biggest slime machine EVER."

After school, Yuck borrowed more bandages from Nurse Payne and went to Cuddly Corner. He tied all the bandages together to make a superlong conveyor belt and unwound it around the room—up and down and back and forth.

Fartin' Martin, Tom Butts, and Little Eric arrived carrying armfuls of slugs and snails.

"We need lots," Yuck said, emptying his bag.

Fartin' Martin emptied his hat. Tom Butts emptied his shoes. Little Eric emptied his pants.

Slugs and snails

rolled out over the floor—hundreds of them!

Yuck, Fartin' Martin, Tom Butts, and Little Eric loaded them onto the conveyor belt.

"You go at the front, Hero," Yuck said, placing Hero nearest the lettuce. "Show everyone what to do."

"We'll need more buckets," Fartin' Martin said.

They stacked buckets and boxes and pots and jars all around the hut to collect the slime.

Hammie hopped into the wheel and began running.

"That's it, Hammie," Yuck said.

The conveyor belt started to move. The slugs and snails started sliding along it, one after the other. The slime machine began sliming.

"Good night, Hammie. Good night, Hero. Good night, everyone."

Yuck, Fartin' Martin, Tom Butts, and Little Eric clambered through the bandages and out of the hut. Yuck locked the door.

"We'll collect the slime in the morning," he said. "There'll be tons of it—our very own Slime Zone!"

But when Yuck got home, Polly was waiting for him.

"I know what really happened at school today," she said. "There's no such thing as a Slime Monster! And now I have the proof!"

From behind her back she pulled out Yuck's copy of *Oink*.

She opened it to the page with the Slime Monster.

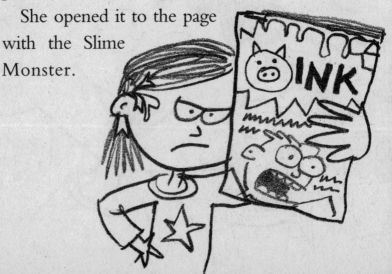

"The Slime Monster's just a story. It's YOU who's been sliming the school!"

"Give me back my *Oink!*" Yuck said, trying to grab his comic from her.

But Polly stuffed it into her bag. "I'm telling on you. You're going to be in BIG TROUBLE."

The next morning, when Yuck left for school, Polly had already gone.

By the time Yuck got there, the Dragon was waiting for him at the school gates. In her hand was his copy of *Oink*.

Standing beside her was Polly.

"You're coming with me," the Dragon said to Yuck, dragging him by his ear to the Reaper's office.

Fartin' Martin, Tom Butts, and Little Eric were already inside.

"I think you have some explaining to do," the Reaper said.

He marched them all to an all-school assembly.

Meanwhile, Polly went to Cuddly Corner to find out what Yuck had been up to. From inside, she could hear strange sounds.

Gurgle! SPLAT! PLOp! SPLASH!

Something was leaking out under the door—slime!

Polly turned the handle, but the door was locked. She rattled and tugged.

Then all at once the door burst open. . . .

A river of slime poured out from Cuddly Corner, knocking Polly to the ground. It covered her from head to toe.

Slime dripped from her hair and oozed from her clothes. She could feel slugs in her socks and snails in her pants.

Hammie the hamster ran across her slimy face.

Hero slimed across her lips.

"Help!" she cried, trying to get up. "HELP!"

But no one heard her. Everyone was in the auditorium.

"There is no such thing as a Slime Monster," the Reaper was saying to the school. "There is no reason for any of you to be afraid. And now we have the proof!"

The Reaper held up Yuck's copy of *Oink*, opening it to the page with the Slime Monster.

"The Slime Monster is a lie," the Reaper said. "It's just a story in a comic belonging to a naughty boy."

He stared straight at Yuck. "Is this yours?"

"Can I have it back, please?" Yuck asked.

"It's you, Yuck! You're the one who's sliming the school!" the Reaper yelled.

Everyone was quiet.

Yuck looked at the Reaper. "I told you, sir. It isn't me." Then Yuck looked around the room. "It's the Slime Monster!"

Everyone gasped.

The Reaper's face turned red with rage. He shouted at Yuck: "THERE IS NO SUCH THING AS A SLIME MONSTER!"

At that moment the doors at the back of the auditorium banged open.

Everyone turned.

Standing in the doorway was a THING—
like a human being, but slimier and scarier. It
walked slowly forward, its arms held out in
front of it, slime dripping from its body and
squelching under its feet.

It tried to speak—"HELP!"—but great
globs of slime spewed from its lips.

"It's the Slime Monster!" everyone
screamed.

Yuck picked up his copy of *Oink* and slipped it into his pocket. He was laughing. "Run for your lives!"

YUCK'S
GROSS
PARTY

Polly Princess stirred the cake batter in the bowl.

Yuck looked at it. It was gooey and chocolatey. He scooped out a sticky dollop and stuffed it into his mouth.

"Hands off!" Polly said. "It's mine."

She bashed him with the spoon.

"Go away!" she said. "It's MY birthday cake for MY birthday party. And YOU'RE not invited!"

Polly poured the cake mixture into a baking pan.

"But I like cake," Yuck said. He licked his fingers.

"Tough!" Polly said. "Because you're not getting any. And you're not coming to my birthday party!"

"Move out of the way, please, Yuck," Mom said, opening the kitchen door.

"Mom, why can't I come to Polly's party?" Yuck asked.

"Because you're gross," Polly said.

"Because last year you ate too much cake and threw up on Polly's presents," Mom told him.

Mom picked up the pan with the cake batter and slid it into the oven.

Yuck took the mixing bowl with the leftover batter and sneaked out of the kitchen. He crept past Dad, who was blowing up party balloons, and ran up the stairs to his room. He sat on his bed, put the bowl on his head, and spun it around, licking it clean.

Yuck decided that when he was EMPEROR OF EVERYTHING he would have the best party ever—a GROSS PARTY! Everyone would be invited. They'd wear gross costumes and play gross games with slime and slugs and mud and maggots. They'd jump around and eat SO MUCH chocolate cake that everyone would be sick!

Yuck set to work on his plan.

At about three o'clock the doorbell rang.

It was Juicy Lucy with Little Eric.

Polly ran to greet her first guests.

"Happy Birthday, Polly," Juicy Lucy said, stepping inside.

"What's he doing here?" Polly asked, pointing at Little Eric.

"I'm here for the party," Little Eric said.

"But you weren't invited."

Yuck appeared at the top of the stairs.

"Not YOUR party, Polly. MY party. It's up here, Eric," he called.

Little Eric ran upstairs.

Juicy Lucy handed Polly a big present wrapped in pink paper. "I didn't know Yuck was having a party too," she said.

"Neither did I!" Polly replied.

The doorbell rang again.
It was Madison Snake.
"Happy Birthday, Polly!"
Madison Snake said. She
was carrying an even bigger
present.

"Thank you," Polly said, taking it from
her with both hands. "I'm going to open
them later."

Madison Snake and Juicy Lucy went into
the living room where Mom poured them
soda. Polly waited by the door as the rest of
her friends arrived—Emily Brush, Clip-Clop
Chloe, Megan the Mouth, Spoiled Jessica,
and Frilly Milly, each carrying a present.

Polly was about to close the door when . . . "Oh no!"

Tom Butts and Fartin' Martin came walking up the path.

"We're here for the party," they said.

"You're not invited," Polly told them.

"Not YOUR party, Polly. MY party!" Yuck called from the top of the stairs.

Fartin' Martin and Tom Butts ran up to Yuck's room.

"I had to hide everything," Yuck said. From his wardrobe Yuck took out three toilet paper rolls, a bottle of ketchup, a tube of toothpaste, a packet of Blowers' Bubblegum and a supersize bottle of Coola Cola.

He popped a piece of bubblegum into his mouth, glugged some Coola Cola, and chewed.

BUUUUURP!

A cola-colored bubblegum bubble expanded from Yuck's lips.

He took it out and stuck it to the wall.

"Balloons!" he said, handing everyone some gum.

They drank and chewed and burped, sticking up Bubblegum Burp Balloons.

Little Eric and Tom Butts decorated the room with streamers, throwing toilet paper rolls back and forth. Fartin' Martin squirted toothpaste onto the ceiling so that it hung down like ribbons. Yuck took the ketchup and squeezed the words "GROSS PARTY" onto the window. In no time at all, the room was ready.

GROSS PARTY

"Welcome to my party!" Yuck said.

He put on some music, and the four of them drank the Coola Cola and jumped around, crashing into one another.

Downstairs, Polly was sitting in the middle of the living room surrounded by a huge pile of presents.

The ceiling thumped.

"Is Yuck having a party too?" Clip-Clop Chloe asked.

"Not a real one," Polly said.

Her friends sat in a circle and watched as Polly opened her presents—a matching Donna Disco skirt and top, pink lip gloss, a *Sparkle* poster, a charm bracelet, a secret diary, and a *Glitter Girl* calendar.

Mom and Dad stood smiling in the doorway.

"Who wants to play a party game?" Polly asked.

Upstairs, Yuck, Fartin' Martin, Tom Butts, and Little Eric crashed down in a big burping heap on the floor.

"Present time!" Yuck said. From under his bed he took out three parcels. "At my party, everyone gets a present."

Fartin' Martin got a fat, slimy slug.

"I call him THE BEAST!" Yuck said.

Fartin' Martin put the slug under his hat for safekeeping.

Tom Butts unwrapped a set of plastic fangs.

"I found them in the park," Yuck told him.

Tom Butts slipped them into his mouth.

Little Eric unwrapped his present.

"Awesome, a stink bomb!" he said.

Yuck's present was a small blob of chocolate cake batter that he'd been keeping on his chin. He licked it.

"Let's get some food," he said.

Yuck, Fartin' Martin, Tom Butts, and Little Eric crept downstairs and peered around the living room door.

"Who wants to play Party Faces?" Polly was asking.

"Can I use your new lip gloss?" Juicy Lucy asked.

"I brought some glitter," Frilly Milly said.

Polly saw Yuck at the door. "What are you doing here? You're not invited."

"We're hungry," Yuck told her, looking at the party food laid out on the table.

"Tell them to go away, Mom!"

"You can each take a small plateful and eat it upstairs," Mom said. "But don't come back for seconds."

Yuck, Little Eric, Fartin' Martin, and Tom Butts each piled a paper plate with chips, sandwiches, cookies, Jell-O, and ice cream.

"Hang on. Where's the chocolate cake?"
Yuck asked.

"We're having it later," Polly said. "And
you're not getting any."

Yuck stuffed a bottle of Coola Cola
under his T-shirt, and they ran back upstairs.

"And now for the party games!" Yuck said.

He opened a cheese sandwich and dolloped in some Jell-O.

"The first game is called Spin and Be Sick."

Everyone ate their food as quickly as possible, stuffing their mouths with Jell-O-filled sandwiches, ice cream, cookies, and chips. They guzzled the Coola Cola.

"Now, SPIN!" Yuck said.

Everyone stood up and began spinning.

"Faster!" Yuck called. "First to be sick is the winner."

They held their arms out and spun around and around, faster and faster.

"I feel dizzy," Tom Butts said.

"I feel giddy," Fartin' Martin said.

"I feel sick," Little Eric said. His stomach was gurgling. "Quick, shake me up!"

The others picked Little Eric up and shook him.

"That's it," he said. "Shake harder!"

Yuck, Fartin' Martin, and Tom Butts turned Little Eric upside down.

Little Eric opened his mouth. "Here it comes!"

BLURGH!

Sandwiches and
ice cream, Jell-O and
cookies and chips fell with a
splash onto the floor.

"I win!" Little Eric said.

Yuck handed Little Eric a
prize—a Superspy Magnifying Glass that had
come free with _Oink_.

Everyone gathered round and inspected
the barf.

"Is that a jelly doughnut?" Tom Butts said.
"I didn't get a jelly doughnut."

"Time for our costumes!" Yuck said.

Tom Butts wrapped a towel around his
shoulders like a vampire cape. Fartin' Martin
wound himself in toilet paper like a mummy.
Yuck stuck a plastic eye to his forehead like
a monster.

Little Eric put on a pair of swimming

goggles from Yuck's drawer. "Is there a prize for the best costume?" he asked.

Yuck nodded. "There's a rubber scorpion for the winner."

"Then watch this," Little Eric said.

Everyone watched as Little Eric opened Yuck's desk and dipped his head in Slime City. He pulled it out, and shiny green slime dripped down his face. "I'm an alien from the planet Xarg!" he said.

The vampire, the mummy, and the monster all laughed. "You look like a frog!"

Little Eric sat down—straight into his barf. "I don't care," he said. He smiled. "This is a great party, Yuck. Much better than Polly's."

Downstairs, Polly and her friends were playing Lucky Dip, sitting in a circle around a big jar of Lucky Lollipops, each of which was wrapped in a Lucky Promise.

Polly pulled out a lollipop and unwrapped it. "You will be rich," she read.

Juicy Lucy pulled out a lollipop. "You will be famous," she read.

"My turn," Megan the Mouth said.

Upstairs, Yuck took out his Disgusting Dip—a huge jar filled with writhing mealworms and disgusting dares.

Fartin' Martin, Tom Butts, and Little Eric dipped their hands in.

"It feels warm and tickly," Tom Butts said.

He pulled out his dare—a hairy ball of belly-button fluff. Stuck to it was a note saying "LICK ME."

"It took me a month to grow that," Yuck said.

Tom Butts held the fluff up to his mouth, stuck his tongue out, and gave it a big lick. "UURRGGHH!"

Little Eric pulled out a bag of chips saying "EAT ME." Inside were pieces of raw onion. He picked out a handful and chewed them. Tears ran down his face. "Eye-watering!"

Yuck's dare was a small box that said "SNIFF ME." He opened it and sniffed.

"There's nothing in it!" the others said.

Yuck held it under their noses.

"PHWOOOAAARRR! What is it?" they asked.

"Cat fart," Yuck told them.

"My turn," Fartin' Martin said. He pulled

out a little container that said "PUT
ME DOWN YOUR PANTS."

Inside was a large, hairy spider.

Fartin' Martin pulled out the elastic
of his pants and popped the spider in.

"It tickles," he said.

He started wriggling.

"You look like you're dancing," Little
Eric said.

Little Eric, Tom Butts, and Yuck stood up
and began shaking their legs and wriggling in
time with Fartin' Martin, doing the
Spiderpants Dance.

In the living room, Polly's friends were whispering to one another.

"What's going on up there?" Frilly Milly asked.

"It sounds like they're dancing again," Megan the Mouth said.

"Why can't we have dancing?" Frilly Milly said. "I love dancing."

"So do I," Clip-Clop Chloe said, clip-clopping her feet up and down.

"Only if I choose the music," Polly told them.

Upstairs, Yuck reached under his bed and took out a rotten apple with holes in it. "This game's called Find the Mealworm," he said.

Yuck put the apple on the floor and spun it round.

"There's a prize for whoever finds a mealworm," he said.

Everyone took turns nibbling the apple.

On his second nibble, Fartin' Martin felt something crawling in his mouth. He opened wide. A mealworm was wriggling on his tongue. "I win!" he said. "What's the prize?"

Yuck picked up the nibbled apple, and from it popped the heads of a dozen more mealworms.

"You get to take all the mealworms home," he said, laughing.

Downstairs, Polly was dancing. "Follow me. Step to the left. Step to the right—"

She turned around. Her friends were sitting down whispering to one another.

Polly turned off the music.

"What's the matter?" she asked.

"We want to do something fun," Spoiled Jessica said.

"I know, let's do my Treasure Hunt," Polly told them.

"What's the treasure?" Spoiled Jessica asked.

"A big bar of chocolate!" Polly said.

Everyone quickly jumped up when they heard this.

"You have to hunt around the house to find it. Ready, set, go!"

Everyone ran out of the living room, pushing past one another.

Upstairs, Yuck opened his desk and took out three slugs from Slime City. "The next game's a race," he said. "A slug race!"

He gave a slug each to Tom Butts and Little Eric. "I'm going to use Hero," he said, taking out his favorite slug. "You can use THE BEAST," he said to Fartin' Martin.

Fartin' Martin took the fat, slimy slug from under his hat.

Yuck squeezed toothpaste in lines across the carpet to make a racetrack. He squeezed a start and finish line at either end. "First slug to cross the line wins a big bar of chocolate," he said.

Yuck stood on his bed and from his dusty shelf took down a giant bar of Chocoblock.

"Wow, where did you get that?" Little Eric asked.

"I found it in the closet under the stairs," Yuck said.

Everyone put their slugs on the start line.

"Ready! Set! Go!"

Little Eric's slug was first away.

Hero went sideways.

Tom Butts's slug went backward. "Wrong way!" Tom Butts shouted.

"Come on," Little Eric cheered.

THE BEAST started eating the toothpaste.

"Not now, BEAST!" Fartin' Martin said, prodding his fat, slimy slug.

"You can't use your hands," Yuck said. "You're only allowed to move your slug with your nose."

At that moment, there was a knock at the door.

"Who's there?" Yuck asked.

"It's Chloe."

Yuck sat on the Chocoblock as Clip-Clop Chloe opened the door.

"Sorry to disturb you," she said, "but I'm hunting for a big bar of chocolate."

"It's not in here," Yuck said.

Clip-Clop Chloe looked at the slugs and toothpaste on the carpet.

"What are you doing?" she asked.

"We're having a party," Fartin' Martin said.

"Why's Little Eric covered in slime?"

"Because it's a GROSS PARTY, the best party ever," Little Eric told her.

"It looks like fun," Clip-Clop Chloe said.

"Chloe!" Polly called from downstairs. "Where are you?"

"Got to go," Chloe said.

She closed the door and clip-clopped down the stairs.

Little Eric's slug was way out in front. He was nudging it along with his nose. Then all of a sudden his slug stopped. Little Eric had pushed it into his barf.

"I'm coming past!" Yuck said, as Hero took the lead.

"No one beats THE BEAST!" Fartin' Martin said. He sneezed, and THE BEAST flew over the FINISH line. "I win!"

Fartin' Martin held up the Chocoblock. "Who wants a piece?"

Downstairs, Polly's friends were gathered in a huddle.

"What kind of person has a treasure hunt with no treasure?" Emily Brush whispered.

"This party is no fun at all," Spoiled Jessica said.

"I promise there was chocolate—a giant bar of Chocoblock. I hid it in the closet under the stairs. I promise I did," Polly said.

"Maybe we should all go home," Madison Snake whispered.

"No, please don't go! We've still got Pass

the Present. Then after that we can have some cake!"

Polly picked up a big present wrapped in layer upon layer of pink paper.

"Mom," she called.

Mom came in from the kitchen and turned the music on. Everyone sat in a circle passing the present between them. When the music stopped, whoever was holding the present tore off a layer of wrapping paper.

Upstairs, Yuck fetched a bucket of mud from his wardrobe. "Who wants to play Pass the Mud?" he asked.

He put some music on, and they passed the bucket around.

"When I stop the music, whoever's holding the bucket scoops out a handful of mud," Yuck said.

"This mud smells," Fartin' Martin said, sniffing his fingers.

"I got it from the garden," Yuck told him.

"Where the cat likes to hang out."

Little Eric scooped out a handful and sniffed it.

Tom Butts scooped out a handful and threw it at Little Eric.

Yuck scooped out a handful and threw it at Tom Butts.

At the bottom of the bucket was a prize. Little Eric got it.

He pulled it out and scraped the mud off. "A bubble machine! Fantastic!"

Downstairs, Polly and her friends were on the last layer of wrapping paper.

The music stopped and the present landed on Spoiled Jessica's lap.

She unwrapped it carefully. "It smells," she said.

"It smells a lot," Megan the Mouth said. The prize was brown. Spoiled Jessica prodded it with her finger.

"IT'S MUD!" she screamed.

"It can't be!" Polly said. "It was supposed to be a bubble machine!"

Upstairs, bubbles were filling Yuck's room. Everyone was leaping around, bursting them.

"Yuck!" Polly screamed, running up the stairs.

Yuck wedged a chair against his door.

"Where's my bubble machine? And where's my chocolate?" Polly shouted, rattling the handle. "Open up and give me back my prizes."

"I don't know what you're talking about, Polly," Yuck said.

Polly stomped down the stairs. "I'm telling Mom!"

But when she got to the living room, everyone had their coats on.

"No, wait," Polly told them. "Don't go."

She handed everyone a paper plate. "Have some food."

While Polly's friends were eating Jell-O and ice cream, Yuck came running in. "We're still hungry. Can we have some more food?" he asked.

"No," Polly said. "Go away."

"You've had yours, Yuck," Mom said. "We don't want you getting sick."

Yuck sneaked off and took a look in the kitchen.

On a huge plate on the table was the big chocolate birthday cake. And on its top the word "Polly" was written in icing, with icing sugar sprinkled over it.

It looked very tasty.

"Wow!" the others said when he came back upstairs.

He placed the cake on his bedroom floor.

"Won't Polly mind?" Little Eric asked.

"We'll just have one slice each," Yuck said, "and then we'll put it back."

But the cake was REALLY tasty.

"Maybe one more slice won't hurt," Fartin' Martin said, passing the cake around again.

They were onto their fourth slice each when Mom knocked on the door.

"Have you seen Polly's cake?" she called.

Everyone looked at the plate on Yuck's floor. There was nothing but crumbs left.

Yuck held the door closed. "It's not in here, Mom," he said.

"What are we going to do?" Tom Butts whispered.

"We're going to be in BIG TROUBLE," Little Eric said.

"Quick, help me," Yuck told them. He grabbed the bucket from Pass the Mud. "Fill it with anything you can find."

Yuck poured the mealworms from the Disgusting Dip into the bottom of the bucket. Tom Butts squeezed in some toothpaste. Fartin' Martin scraped up some slug slime from the floor.

Everyone stared.

"Are you sure?" Little Eric said.

SPLAT! In it went.

Yuck sloshed everything around, churning the mixture with his hand. "We need something chocolatey."

They threw in handfuls of mud.

Yuck took down the Bubblegum Burp Balloons and dropped them in. **BURP! BURP! BURP!** Fartin' Martin pulled a spider's web from his pants and dropped that in. Tom Butts stirred his belly-button fluff into the mixture. Little Eric added some raw onions, then scraped the slime from his head.

"Eye-watering slime," he said.

Then Yuck plopped in some ketchup and boogers and a final scoop of mud. The mixture was a thick chocolate brown.

Yuck turned the bucket upside down

onto the plate and patted the bottom.

He lifted the bucket off, and there it was . . . Polly's brand-new birthday cake.

On the top of the cake he wrote "Polly" in toothpaste.

Then he shook his head over it, sprinkling dandruff like icing sugar.

"Good enough to eat," Fartin' Martin said.

"Wait. A birthday cake should have candles," Little Eric said.

Yuck took a pot from beside his bed.

It was marked YUCK'S EARWAX—DO NOT TOUCH.

He scooped a handful of wax from the pot. It was yellow with brown bits in it. He rolled the earwax into candles and put a piece of string in the top of each. Then he tiptoed downstairs to the kitchen, put the new cake in the fridge, and ran back up to his room.

It was Dad who found it.

"It's in the fridge, dear!"

"Oh, how lovely," Mom said, "you've added some candles. Polly will be thrilled."

Polly smiled as Mom and Dad carried the cake into the living room.

Her friends gathered round in a circle . . .

"Happy Birthday to you! Happy Birthday to you! Happy Birthday, dear Polly! Happy Birthday to you!"

The candles flickered and sputtered bright green flames.

Polly took a deep breath and . . .

"Make a wish, Polly!" Juicy Lucy said.

Polly closed her eyes and blew.

"I wish everyone would stay," she said.

"You're not supposed to say it out loud or it won't come true," Emily Brush told her.

Yuck, Little Eric, Tom Butts, and Fartin' Martin crept down to the living room door and watched as Mom cut everyone a big slice of cake.

"There's a piece for each of you," Polly said, handing the plates out.

Yuck giggled in the doorway.

"What are YOU doing here, Yuck?" Polly said to him. "You're not invited!"

"I just came to say happy birthday," Yuck told her.

"Well, you can't have any cake," Polly said. "It's ALL for us!"

Yuck smiled as a slice of cake wriggled on Polly's plate.

"Eat up, everyone," Polly said. "I made it myself."

Yuck watched as one by one each of Polly's friends took a bite.

Their noses curled upward.

Cake slithered through their fingers. It crawled from their nostrils and wriggled down their chins.

Their cheeks filled as they puked.

Madison Snake puked on Frilly Milly.

Frilly Milly puked on Megan the Mouth.

Megan the Mouth puked on Spoiled Jessica.

Spoiled Jessica puked on Juicy Lucy.

Juicy Lucy puked on Clip-Clop Chloe.

Clip-Clop Chloe puked on Emily Brush.

Emily Brush puked on Madison Snake.

Polly was sitting in the middle.

"How does it taste?" Yuck asked her.

BLURGH!

Polly puked on her presents.

"Did you eat too much, Polly?" Yuck asked.

But Polly didn't reply. Cake was crawling all over her face.

"That's gross," Yuck said. "What a GROSS PARTY!"

LAUGH YOUR SOCKS OFF WITH YUCK, THE BOY WHO LOVES BUGS AND SLUGS AND SLIME.

YUCK'S AMAZING UNDERPANTS

Yuck has been wearing his favorite underpants every day and every night for *six weeks*. Mom wants them washed ASAP, but Yuck has other plans. . . .

YUCK'S SCARY SPIDER

Yuck's spider is big, fat, and hairy, and everyone at school is scared of it. But Yuck knows his spider is only trying to be friendly. When the principal traps the spider under a glass in his office, it's Yuck to the rescue!